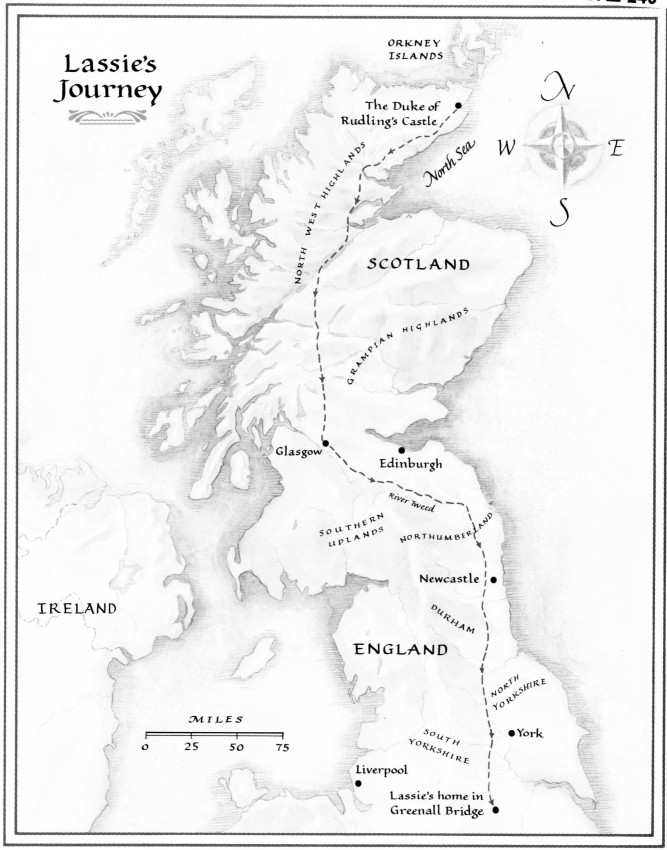

For Helen and Jim –R. W.   For Midge and Albert Cook –S. J.

Henry Holt and Company, LLC, *Publishers since 1866*, 175 Fifth Avenue, New York, New York 10010 [www.HenryHoltKids.com]. Henry Holt ® is a registered trademark of Henry Holt and Company, LLC. Text copyright © 1995 by Rosemary Wells. Illustrations copyright © 1995 by Susan Jeffers. Map by Claudia Carlson. Based on *Lassie Come-Home* by Eric Knight / Copyright © 1940 by Jere Knight. Copyright renewed © 1968 by Jere Knight, Betty Noyes Knight, Winifred Knight Mewborn, and Jennie Knight Moore. First published as a short story in the *Saturday Evening Post*. Copyright © 1938 by the Curtis Publishing Company. Copyright renewed © 1966 by Jere Knight, Betty Noyes Knight, Winifred Knight Mewborn, and Jennie Knight Moore. All rights reserved. Distributed in Canada by H. B. Fenn and Company Ltd. Library of Congress Cataloging-in-Publication Data: Wells, Rosemary. Eric Knight's Lassie come-home: the original 1938 classic / written for young readers by Rosemary Wells; illustrated by Susan Jeffers. Summary: Sold in financial desperation to a wealthy duke, a collie undertakes a 1000-mile journey in order to be reunited with her former master in Yorkshire. 1. Dogs—Juvenile fiction. [1. Dogs—Fiction.] I. Jeffers, Susan, ill. II. Knight, Eric Mowbray, 1897–1943. Lassie come-home. III. Title. PZ10.3.W486Er 1995 [Fic]—dc20 95-6064 ISBN 978-0-8050-5995-3 First hardcover edition published in 1995 by Henry Holt and Company. First paperback edition—1998. Printed in August 2009 in China by South China Printing Company Ltd., Dongguan city, Guangdong Province, on acid-free paper. ∞ The artist used watercolor, ink, and pencil on Arches aquarelle paper to create the illustrations for this book.

5 7 9 11 13 15 14 12 10 8 6

Thanks to Sigi Allen, Lucinda Barton, Steve Cook, Becky Goodman, Beezoo Wells, Victoria Wells, and Debhill Bontaw Dreams Legacy CDX, the collie who posed for Lassie.

ERIC KNIGHT'S ORIGINAL 1938 CLASSIC

Lassie Come-Home

In a New Picture-Book Edition
Written for Young Readers
by Rosemary Wells

Illustrations by Susan Jeffers

Henry Holt and Company · New York

PART ONE

She was sable, black, and snow white. Her amber eyes lit up the face of anyone who looked into them. All the village of Greenall Bridge said Lassie was the best collie they'd ever seen.

One May morning, without telling anyone, Joe's father sold Lassie for fifteen pounds, ten shillings. He sold her because he'd lost his job for good. This was more than three weeks' wages.

How would he tell his son, Joe? What would Joe do when he found Lassie not waiting for him as she always did after school?

When Joe saw the grassy corner of the schoolyard empty that afternoon at four, a panic rose in the back of his mouth. Greenall Bridge was a quiet village, and Joe knew perfectly well Lassie had neither been run over or stolen. Before he even ran to ask his mother what had happened, a corner of his heart darkened.

He dashed home. Clattering into the kitchen, he shouted, "Mother, something's happened to Lassie! Where is she? She wasn't at school!"

Joe's mother said, "She's sold. That's what, and there isn't any good you trying to change it."

"Sold!" said Joe.

"Sold," repeated his mother. "Come sit down for your tea, Joe."

"But how could you sell her . . . how could anyone?" Joe's voice rose like a child's, as words of any sense fell away from him.

Joe's father, usually quiet, knocked over his chair and stormed out of the door. He had not, of course, found a way to tell his son.

Joe sat. His tea and bread might as well have been twigs and leaves.

"Eat, Joe," his mother urged him.

After a time his mother spoke of the closing of the mine where his father worked. She reminded him they could just pay the rent this month and did not have much left over for more than a little bread with no jam and tea with no milk. All the time she talked, she scrubbed and polished.

Joe listened to her talk of the hard times. Her words circled in the way of the Yorkshire villagers. People of that time and place seldom spoke of the hurt and love they felt most deeply.

The kitchen was the center of greatest comfort in Joe's life. Now a twilight had moved in. Lassie was as good as dead, her spot on the hearth empty, her brush on the mantel unused. Joe could not eat to please his mother because his throat was as closed as a fist.

Upstairs in bed Joe tried to make things better in his mind by going over his mother's words. Hundreds of miner fathers losing their jobs. No money for rent. No money for new shoes. No jobs meant a man's weak lungs were treated with homemade steam tents instead of expensive medicine. Women were picking the very weeds from the sheep pastures to boil for soup, not to mention men talking to themselves in broad daylight.

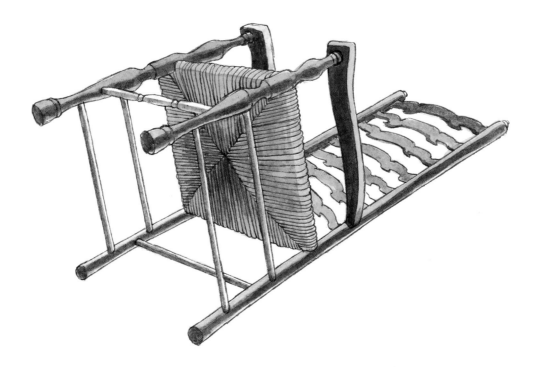

Joe's father came home long after dark. He should have been brushing Lassie now, as he did every night in front of the fire. A hundred scars crisscrossed Joe's father's hands from hacking coal out of a pit six days a week. But in the evenings the same rough hands swam over the collie's coat like a mother's hands on a baby, and fluffed it as silky as a swan.

Joe's father coughed. Coal miners breathed in black dust all day and hacked most of the night. Down in the mines, coal dust hung in every lungful of air and wept in underground rivers down the walls of the mine tunnels. Coal stayed part of the men seven days a week no matter if they scrubbed their hands red-raw for Sunday church.

Yorkshire granddads slept sitting up straight as sticks in bed. None could breathe lying down after a life in the pits.

Children were taught not to whine or cry, and mostly they didn't once they'd passed the age of lost penny-sweets. Joe listened for some change of mind from downstairs, and cried quietly. He swallowed all sounds of tears because he was ashamed.

Lassie was Joe's bright light in a strict grey world. Lassie was the true mate he could talk to in a time when no one said what they really felt, only what they ought to feel. Lassie was Joe's laughter before he would have to grow up and follow his father into the pit.

Joe stood at his window and prayed to God to return his collie, knowing all the while God was not about to cross his parents' will.

Lassie herself was three miles away in a kennel with thirty other dogs. She did not know that her new owner, the Duke of Rudling, had been trying to pry her and buy her from Joe's father for three years.

She longed only to be with the family she loved and out of the iron fence that imprisoned her. Her spirits heavy, she lay still all night.

After he'd bought his new collie, the Duke went riding with his granddaughter, Priscilla. They trotted over old sheep paths and across the meadows, ending their ride in the village. The Duke greeted many of the shopkeepers as he always did, with a tap of his riding crop to his hat. Priscilla noticed a knot of men she'd never seen before standing by the jobs office in the village square. They were waiting sour-faced for any little job to be posted, knowing there was no work for fifty miles around. Her grandfather did not seem to see them.

Over tea she asked him who they were.

"Miners, I expect," said her grandfather.

"What were they doing, Grandfather?" Priscilla asked. She stirred her tea thoughtfully. The solemn faces of the men in the market square worried her.

"Smoking their pipes and wasting the time of day, wouldn't you say?" answered her grandfather, twinkling his eyes at his grand-daughter.

Priscilla chose a different jam from a silver jam spinner every day of the week. Today was raspberry. She slathered it on a scone thickly spread with cream. "Grandfather, your new collie, Lassie, . . . she doesn't look happy. I called her name, but she just lay there as if she were made of stone."

The Duke was annoyed. He'd noticed this as well. In his mind this was the fault of his kennelman, Hynes. "Now that I've bought that dog," grumbled the Duke, "I intend to win some important shows with her. Hynes had better keep her in top form."

The Duke handed Priscilla the silver sugar spoon. It had an amethyst thistle flower set at the end, and Priscilla watched it sparkle in the sunlight. The thistle was the symbol of Scotland and of her grandfather's estate far in the Highlands. She saved part of the scone for Lassie. But when she went out to find her, Lassie was gone.

It was not easy for Joe to keep his mind still. He prepared every nerve in his body for Lassie not to be there when he came out of school, but wonder of wonders, there she was and his stomach leaped like a fish in a stream. "The pit must have reopened! Perhaps father got a new job! The Duke must have changed his mind!" All of these possibilities raced through Joe's head as he ran home.

Then when he threw back the kitchen door and said Lassie's come home and wasn't it the best thing in the world, one look at his mother's face told him it was all a mistake.

Quietly, Lassie crept to the hearth tail-down, as if she had caused all the trouble. She put her muzzle on Joe's father's boot, but he pulled his foot away. She nudged his hand and he yanked up his arm.

"Back she goes, Joe," said Joe's mother.

There was no more talk because a stranger in riding breeches sauntered into their kitchen. He held a leash before him like a noose.

"Mr. Hynes, is it?" snapped Joe's mother. "I'll thank you to knock and wipe your feet before you come into my kitchen!"

"No surprise your dog's back," said Hynes. "I know you villagers and your come-home dogs. You sell an honest man a dog and train it to dig out and sell it to someone else before the hour's up." He reached for Lassie and she shrank from him.

Hynes could not easily get around Joe's mother. She was his size and then some. "You'll take those words back," she said.

Joe's father placed the leash on his collie's neck himself, led her trembling out to the roadway, and handed her over to Hynes without a word.

"Red-eared bully," sputtered Joe's mother loud enough for Hynes to hear, "parading into my kitchen as if it were a public house."

Hynes led Lassie away. "You'll never get away from me again, my dear. I'll see to that!" he scolded.

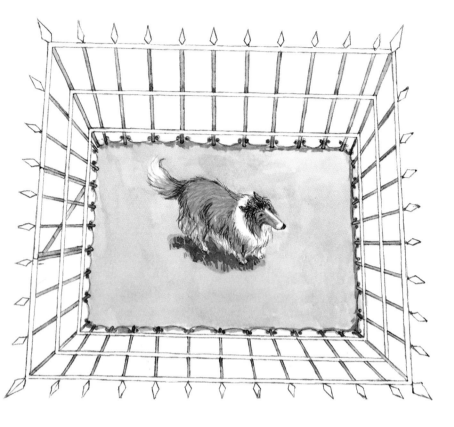

Dogs have a sense of time truer than any clock of man's making. The following day, just before four, the time sense woke in Lassie. She began to pace in her kennel and dig out under the barricades that Hynes had piled against the wire. At four o'clock she was waiting for Joe at school.

This time Joe was determined to make his parents listen.

But listen they did not, any more than a stone listens to the wind, and Joe knew he couldn't change things even if he argued all night long.

"We have taken the Duke's money, lad," said Joe's father. "We have spent it and she's not ours to keep."

All the same, Joe's mother made Lassie a proper supper because she said she looked poorly, and Joe's father took up her brush and made her coat glow and dance in the firelight, as was the greatest pleasure of all his days before. For a moment Joe believed that all was well and the terrible darkness had moved on. Then his father's face set grimly and he said, "Come, Joe. We must take her back. It's you she comes home for, and it's you must tell her to stay and not plague us."

A fog chilled the winding track that took them to Rudling Hall. Joe's hand trailed along the tops of Lassie's velvet ears. There were many stories told in the village of the Duke's amazing wealth. Whether they were true or not Joe didn't know, but he spoke in anger to his father that the balance of things between rich and poor was unfair.

"It's the way of the world," said his father, sucking on a pipe empty of tobacco.

From behind a juniper tree Priscilla watched Joe and his father bring Lassie back to the kennels. She heard her grandfather bellow at Hynes for allowing Lassie to escape.

She saw Joe's father's hand at the back of Joe's shoulders poking him, making the boy put his dog in the kennel. Making him fasten the gate. Making him say good-bye. She heard Joe's words to Lassie in a voice that was hardly a boy's voice at all, but gruff like an old man's.

"Stay, girl. Never, never come back to us. We don't want you home anymore."

Lassie did not recognize these words. But she smelled fear and grief all around the boy and man she loved.

Priscilla watched Joe, blinded with tears, turn away from his dog. Joe's father was embarrassed by this, she guessed, because he pushed his boy along. When father and son were out of sight, Priscilla reached both arms through the fence and called to Lassie. But there was no catching the dog's eye or stopping the terrible cry that came from her.

Hynes worked over Lassie's pen as if it contained a bull. The next day at four she dug in all the places she'd tried before, but rocks had been set all around. She tried to jump, but the fence was six feet and collies are poor jumpers. Still the time sense pulsed like a second heart beating, and she threw herself at the corner of the pen and hooked her front legs over the top before tumbling back. On the next try she climbed and within a minute she was free.

The moors of Yorkshire are sweeps of rock as big and tilting as the sea. The shallow soil allows just a knuckle-deep layer of tough grass and bracken to grow. Sheep graze them and mine tunnels have been dug in them, but you cannot know the moors until you walk them yourself.

Joe's father had been a boy here. He knew all the twisting paths that doubled you back where you started. He knew doors into the very earth itself and the ways familiar only to rabbits and village children.

He found Joe and Lassie in a far place where the boulders lay toppled like giant chessmen. He sat beside his son and ran his hand through his collie's mane, damp from the mist outside, into the dry, warm undercoat. Jamming his pipe between his teeth, he patted all his pockets for his tobacco pouch.

"Father," said Joe quietly, "please don't make her go back. Please, Father."

His father was not a talky man. "Time I stopped smoking. No good for me anyway," he grunted at last.

"Father, please."

"Joe, we've spent the Duke's brass. She's not ours to keep."

"But Father," Joe began again, "you cannot buy or sell—" Joe was so uncomfortable using the word *love* in front of his father that he couldn't say it.

"We've nothing left. Not a farthing. Or I wouldn't have done it."

"Nothing left?" asked Joe.

"Nothing," said his father, and he tossed his pipe over the rocks and it fell in a crevice. "A roof over our heads. A little bread with no jam. A little tea with no milk, and honesty. Honesty we have left. Swallow this sadness, now, Joe. Be a man and take it."

Joe held Lassie's muzzle under his chin. His arm circled her shoulders and chest and met his father's hand on the other side. Together they leaned against the in-and-out of her breathing.

Joe wanted to say, "Is being a man choosing a few tins of milk over what loves you and needs you?" But in his father's steel-blue eyes was no softness or give, and Joe said nothing.

After a little while the three went back across the moors the way they had come.

In a week's time his mother grabbed Joe by the shoulders. Looking square at him, she told him, "Finish your supper. You're worrying your father to death, eating like a sparrow. Lassie's not coming home again, Joe. Get that into your head. The Duke's taken her up to Scotland to stay."

"Scotland!"

"Scotland, Joe. Away in the mountains, the Highlands. Eight hundred miles. Farther than you'll ever go in this life or any other."

Joe tried to forget. But many a day he gazed at the clouds that gathered low against the horizon to the north. He knew they were only clouds but pretended they were mountains all the same, pretended that Scotland was just there where he could see it.

PART TWO

The journey to the north of Scotland was two and a half days by
fast train. Lassie lay in her kennel unaware of how far she was
from her home. Hynes peered at the map over his bunk, and counted
the miles off as they flew past under the thundering wheels of the
Highland Express.

When at last he led Lassie out of her kennel, he spotted the home-
sickness in her eyes as she took in the unfamiliar countryside.

"You'll not get home so easy again, Yer Majesty," he said. "You
could run your heart out to kingdom come and not go half an inch on
the map of Scotland."

Lassie understood only the cruel jokiness in his voice.

The Duke's castle, frowning out upon the islands of the North Sea, did not smell any righter than his Yorkshire estate. Worse, Hynes chained her inside her kennel run. There she stayed for three weeks.

If Hynes were ever to blame anyone for what happened next, it would have to be Priscilla.

To begin with, it was Priscilla who asked, as they mounted up for their afternoon ride, "Grandfather, why is that poor collie on a chain in her pen? She cries horribly and her pretty eyes are all sad and dull."

The Duke swung right off his horse and stomped out to the dog runs. He roared at Hynes. "No dog of mine sits at the end of a chain, thank you very much, Mr. Hynes! Take her out and give her some exercise. This minute, man."

The only part of the castle grounds not enclosed by a ten-foot stone wall was where the land ended in a cliff over the crashing sea below. Hynes marched Lassie up and down a path planted with cedars, growing at crippled angles from the North Sea wind. He jerked her leash. "Yer Majesty needs some exercise!" he lisped angrily at her.

Lassie stopped short. She didn't understand.

"Come along, for pity's sake," said Hynes, jerking her again. "My tea's gone nice and cold, thanks to you."

It was Hynes's bad luck that it was just teatime, four o'clock. Of course he had no idea what four o'clock meant to Lassie. Quite suddenly it was time . . . time to go for the boy. In the space of half a second she ducked her head out of the leash and was free. Hynes followed her, sweating and swearing under his breath. The kennelman's job at six pounds a week and the cozy cottage that went with it were up in smoke if he didn't get her back. He reckoned he could corner her easily, since there was only a single gate in the whole enclosure of the castle grounds.

It happened that Priscilla was always the one to dismount and open the gate, and so she did now. Over her shoulder she saw Lassie bounding toward them and heard Hynes shouting, "Miss Priscilla! Close that gate! Close that gate!"

Priscilla very nearly did, but in her mind's eye lingered a picture of the village boy bent over the head of his beloved collie, crooning, "Stay, girl. Never, never come back to us. We don't want you home anymore." All the while his fingers plowing through her coat and his heart breaking in his voice.

Lassie was at that moment running full tilt toward the gate.

"Close that gate, Miss Priscilla!" Hynes ordered sharply.

"Good luck, girl!" Priscilla cried, and slammed the gate shut in Hynes's face a second after Lassie swept through it.

"What was that you wanted, Mr. Hynes?" she asked him with a smile as wide as the month of July.

No one knows just why animals feel a pull toward their homes, but it is part of their mystery to us. It took Lassie only a moment smelling the wind, and then she headed due south.

She trotted through the village that in the old days had served the Duke's estate. Suddenly two men crowded her path.

"That's a champion collie or my name's Queen Mary," said one of the men to his mate.

The mate agreed. "Probably one of the Duke's show dogs. Sure as eggs is eggs there's a reward for her."

Stubby fingers snatched at Lassie's mane. She darted away, dodging a thrown rock. She did not understand why the hands of men, once so friendly, had turned against her, but she would avoid them from now on. She galloped on away to the hills.

In the summer a soft heather blanket covers the stony crags of the Scottish Highlands. Here and there you might see a cottage off on its own, but the sky goes on forever and the land knows no end. Into this country Lassie fled.

She did not eat until the fourth day out, when she startled a weasel into dropping a fresh-killed rabbit. She ate it delicately, being accustomed only to food in a dish, but from then on she learned quickly to hunt when she was hungry.

There was poor shelter in the raw nights. She slept beneath rocks, stomach growling in the cold. Thunderstorms frightened her. Farm dogs snarled at her. Burrs tangled in her coat. Lassie turned grubby, thin, and footsore after a week and only sixty miles. With the great patience that animals have to bear pain and hunger, she had only one thing in her mind: south, ever south, toward home.

She kept on a steady pace until one day she found herself at water's edge. It was far too wide to swim across. She did not know that she'd come to the top of the great lochs of Scotland, a string of deep, wide lakes that cut the country nearly in two.

She loped east along the lakeside for a while but could not find a way leading south. She turned west, but it was no better.

In the afternoon a landscape painter, sitting in his boat, saw a collie in the grass beside the loch. He heard from her a howl of such deep mourning that he turned from his canvas, rowed in to shore, and spoke to her. "You're on your way somewhere, girl," he said gently. She looked so forlorn, he gave her the sausages and hard-boiled eggs he'd packed for lunch. She ate it hungrily and then was off, west again, which seemed to have just a bit more south promised in it than the other direction.

Eight weeks and a hundred miles later she was still heading south-west, looking for a way around the endless water. In a front paw a thorn festered. It jabbed at every footfall. In the times when she lay and rested, she chewed at it but it would not come out.

After a long blur of passing time, the lochs narrowed and then dwindled to a river. Lassie tried to judge whether she could cross, smelling the scent of men and machinery downstream. Her beautiful coat lay matted and filthy on her thin sides. Limping, weary, she plunged into the river. The moment she hit its current, the water swallowed her, sucking her downstream like a stick of wood.

Five boys straddled a railway bridge over the river and saw her bobbing, struggling, drowning in the racing white water.

"Look! A dog!" cried one, and immediately they all began hurling stones at her, each trying to hit her and daring the others on.

The current finally drove her to a calm spot. With the last strength in her body she paddled to shore. Water charged up from her stomach and lungs.

When animals are sick in the wild, they pull away within themselves to die or to get better. She dragged herself shivering beneath an old rusted furnace to let the fever course through her. The thorn took a week to work out of the pad of Lassie's forepaw. The infection gone, the fever broke, she struggled to her feet and went on, light-headed with hunger.

A woman walking through the center of Glasgow, the busiest city in Scotland, noticed a heap of ragged fur on the pavement. Lassie lay tangled in a dogcatcher's net. Two men took turns clubbing her.

The woman shoved the men back. She shouted in their faces, "If either of you two savages lays a hand on that dog again, I'll see to it you lose your jobs!"

"That's a filthy mongrel, ma'am," said one of the dogcatchers. "She may bite you. Stay back from her."

"What nonsense!" said the woman. "She's a living creature suffering and you two are a couple of brutes." She undid the cords of the net. Running her hands over Lassie's bony sides, she soothed her into quietness. For a moment Lassie opened her eyes as if to answer this kindness.

"She's starving," said the woman. "You are to take her into the pound and feed her now. I will fetch her in my car in one hour and take her home. Is that clear?"

"Yes, ma'am," said the dogcatchers.

But of course Lassie understood not a word of this. The first

chance she got, she slipped the men's grasp and went out a window onto a fire escape. They came at her with their nets again. She jumped. It was twenty feet to the cobblestones below. She landed yelping with the agony of a separated shoulder.

Holding her injured leg up, she managed to vanish into the city of Glasgow and out its south end. There were no more rabbits in this countryside, and she was too weak to chase them anyway.

She ate a heel of bread one day and a tossed-away sandwich another. She made very slow progress now, always keeping her distance from men. Sleep did not heal her shoulder or ease the sickness that had settled in her chest. Another river blocked her path. She blacked out halfway across. Kindly the water deposited her on its other bank. The river was the Tweed. She did not know it, of course, but she was at last in England.

Her legs wouldn't work when she willed them. Inching along on her belly, she headed toward a small farm cottage, where she smelled food and where the firelight spilled through the cracks in the kitchen door. A dram more strength and Lassie would have pulled herself near enough to be heard by the people inside the cottage.

For the first time, four o'clock passed in a drizzle without her knowing it. The wind blew the chilly rain into her ruined coat. No one noticed her crying, soft as a kitten.

Neither the man nor the woman in the cottage heard anything over the beating of the rain on their roof until just before ten o'clock. The man stirred in bed.

"Did you hear that, Dally?" he whispered in the darkness. "The chickens are fussing."

"Aye," said his wife. "Might be a fox, Dan."

Dally fetched a lantern and an umbrella and held it for Dan. Together they crept out into the sleet.

"Oh, for the love of God, look at that. A collie." Dan placed his arm under Lassie's shoulders. She did not move.

They lay her on the hearth rug and dried her with a potato sack.
Dan stoked up the fire. Dally opened a tin of condensed milk.

"That's the last of the week's milk," he warned her. "You know
you don't like your tea without."

Dally seemed not to hear. Again and again she spooned milk into
Lassie's mouth, only to see it dribble out unswallowed.

"She's too far gone, love," said Dan. "Come away to bed. It's well
past ten."

But at midnight Lassie swallowed. By morning the puzzled eyes
opened and blinked. Dan brought in two eggs from the henhouse.
One he shared with his wife. The other he spoon-fed to Lassie.

The house smelled right. The love of Dan and Dally healed Lassie
as much as their careful feeding. They called her Bonnie.

Dally doted on her new friend. She fed her up and brushed her twice a day. When the weeks went by and Dally was sure no one would claim her, she walked her around the village with such pride as a mother takes in a new baby.

"Bonnie's put roses in your cheeks," Dan said.

"She's done that!" Dally agreed.

"And she's happy with us, don't you think?" Dan asked.

"I think so," answered Dally, "excepting every day at four o'clock. Then she nearly tears the paint off the door to get out. Dan, I believe Bonnie's on her way somewhere."

The next afternoon at a quarter to four, Dally patted her apron and called Lassie to her side. "You've only stopped with us for a wee rest, haven't you, my girl?" She ran her fingers over the sable-and-gold head. "I know, I know," said Dally. "You want to be on your way, don't you?" She opened the door. "I can't see one I love so much in sorrow."

For a moment Lassie paused on the doorsill and glanced back as if for permission.

"Go, my heart's own Bonnie," said Dally. "God be with you."

PART THREE

Every day, a little bit more, Joe had pushed Lassie out of his mind. Mornings when she was not there to run to school with him, he pretended she'd never been. He hid her brush, her dish, the rug that she slept on at the foot of his bed.

He managed well until the Friday before Christmas when a spelling test ran beyond the last bell. In the schoolyard he heard barking. Dropping his pencil he ran to the window. He did not hear the teacher scold him.

It was only a stray terrier in the street below, and the teacher punished him for disrupting the class. At that moment his heart was flooded with every ounce of longing he'd pushed out of it, and now he would have to begin all over again.

The north of England has never been rich country to begin with, and winter is a withering time for creatures out in the cold. Money was as rare as hens' teeth.

There was barely a rind of cheese thrown away in the whole county for a hungry dog to find.

A hundred miles from Greenall Bridge, Lassie thought only of the road from herself to Joe. The better part of a year without food and shelter had nearly destroyed her. Dan and Dally's warm hearth and good food faded as winter dragged along. Her shoulder ached in the long raw nights. Her lungs quit sometimes in the cutting air, and she went only a fraction of the distance she'd covered during the summer.

One evening two sheep farmers saw her cross their meadow.

"Could be the mongrel that's out killing lambs," said one.

"No. It's a collie," said the other.

"Shoot it anyway," said the first farmer. "She don't belong to no one 'round here."

The farmer's own dog smelled Lassie and, streaking over the pasture, attacked her before his master could cock his gun.

Lassie tried to break away, but the big healthy farm dog was too full of energy for her. For five or six minutes he snapped and tore at her, rolling her heavily on her bad side. He very nearly killed her. Suddenly she squirmed out from beneath him and caught him under the mouth. She held him there until he stopped thrashing and then, when he lay still, she let go and slipped quietly away.

"It's no lamb-killing mongrel. That's a purebred collie," said the farmer with the gun. He put his weapon down. "I couldn't shoot anyway. Poor thing. I hope it finds its way home."

Lassie slept that night and the next in a cow barn. She had lost a great deal of blood in the fight. She did not know she was beginning to get pneumonia, and it would be the finish of her unless she found shelter and food. The next morning the farmer's wife came out to milk the cows. Later the woman told her husband, "The poorest dog's been in the barn for three days. I gave her the old horse blanket and fresh milk. Hasn't eaten in a month of Sundays. Gone this morning."

Sixty-odd miles from Greenall Bridge, Lassie slept in deep burrows in the snow, protected from the wind this way. Ice formed between the pads of her feet and numbed all feeling.

One morning a child saw her and gave her half a sausage roll. Another morning she found a grouse trapped in the snow and killed it to eat. The wounds from the dogfight did not heal well. Still she headed south into the dales of Yorkshire, into the dead of February.

March was little better. The rain bucketed down and the wind snapped bitterly from the north for a fortnight. Then one day the sun broke through and she crawled to the right street, to the school-yard, to the gate. And there she lay in the blowing leaves, waiting for him.

Joe could not believe it was his dog. Her name tumbled out of Joe's mouth again and again as he knelt beside her. She could not lift her head, but she thumped her tail up and down and her eyes said, "Here I am. What is so special?"

Joe listened to her lungs rasp shallow in the way of old miners before death took them. Lifting her light body, he carried her up the High Street. "You're my Lassie come-home," Joe said. "My Lassie come-home, and they'll have to pull me limb from limb before they ever take you away again."

When he reached his house and pushed open the door, his father was sitting sewing new soles on his old boots. Until this moment Joe had never seen his father cry.

Joe's mother wrapped Lassie in her winter coat. Using a blanket spread across two chairs, she rigged a tent over the steam kettle the same as she did for Joe's father when he got bad.

In one of the good teacups, wrapped in Christmas paper, were two pills saved for Joe's father's lungs. They had cost five precious shillings. His father crushed them into an eggcup of brandy. With an eyedropper he got the mixture down Lassie's throat.

In the end it was Joe's mother who put it all right. When the supper dishes had been cleared away, she said to her husband, "You are muddling over the right and wrong of this. Now, here's a simple fact. If it was us that needed Lassie, it would not be right to keep her. But it's she, poor thing, that needs us. She's her own self and was never ours to sell in the first place."

Light sparkled in Joe's mother's eyes. "And it'll be over my dead body that Lassie's handed back to that plush-bottomed Duke of Rudling, no matter if he sends ten constables to this house."

Lying beside his collie, Joe tried to will his own energy and health into the slow-breathing body that did not move from the hearth. Lassie cared only that the hands upon her were the right hands and that the voices she heard through the thick fog of pneumonia were the right voices. Over and over Joe said her name and told her secrets that the two of them alone understood.

Priscilla visited her grandfather at her next school holidays. She did not believe her eyes when she saw Lassie at Joe's side, the two of them chasing a rabbit over the meadow.

Her grandfather smiled. "That boy's father is the best dog man in Yorkshire," he said. "I gave him Hynes's job. Hynes's cottage. Six pounds a week I pay him. What do you think of that?"

"Grandfather," said Priscilla. "She must have walked five hundred miles."

"A thousand miles," said the Duke. "And nearly a year to do it."

Then he said, laughing, "I had to buy the man, woman, and boy to get the dog back on my property. Can you imagine? I've bought a man to get a dog!"

Priscilla watched them in the meadow from a window in Rudling Hall. She understood quite well there could be no buying or selling of any living creature.

Eyes bright, Lassie danced at Joe's side. In that tick of time they spoke a language like a song, boy and dog, sun and meadow.